I0757478

Copyright © 2021 by Mary E. Rasamny Esq.
All rights reserved.

This book or any portion thereof may not be reproduced or used in any manner whatsoever without the written permission of the publisher except for the use of brief quotations in a book review.

'*Slomo Sloth*' is a registered trademark of Mary rasamny
U.S. Serial Number 90197383

This book is dedicated to the
newest Little People, Demi,
Drew and Cameron.

A special thank you to Emmy
for the story idea.

SLICK & SLOMO™

A Silly Sloth Story

By Mary Rasamny

Illustrated by Izzy Bean

Hello and welcome!

I hope you enjoy reading this silly sloth story.

Chapter 1
LIFE IN A BASKET

We are a family of stuffed sloths who live in a very crowded basket in the Big People's basement.

We are crammed in there with all kinds of other stuffed animals. My favorites are Owl and Hedgehog because they are quiet and clean, even if Owl is a little bit of a know-it-all and Hedgehog is really prickly. Some of the others, especially Raccoon, are noisy and stinky. Blue Dragon is forever breathing fire in my face and Puppy simply has no sense of personal space and always wants to cuddle. Billy Goat thinks nothing of kicking me in the head and Camel spits in my face for no reason whatsoever! Can you even imagine that? Clearly some of my stuffed friends should learn some manners!

The Mom pulls us out of our basket once in a while like when Little People with their sticky fingers and runny noses come to visit. They like to drape us around their necks or just throw us back and forth like bean bags!

But at least we get to hang upside down and stretch our long arms and legs.

During Christmas the Mom props us up in the kitchen as decorations because we are, in fact, Christmas sloths as you can tell by our hats and sweaters and, of course, by those silly blinking lights on Shee Shee, our little one.

Oh, I should introduce myself: I am Slick Sloth and my wife is Slip Sloth. These are very difficult names to say. You should try it now while I wait; go ahead, try to say our names! I told you so!

It became super clear to us that the Mom was growing more and more obsessed with sloths.

She has a pretty little sloth jewelry dish on her dresser, wears sloth socks to bed, has a full sized sloth sticker on her car window and drinks red wine from her "slothed" wine glass. We take all this as a compliment and try to encourage her by having good behavior!

Our lives in the basement are very uneventful. We sleep most of the day and hang upside down during the night because we are nocturnal and that's what sloths do!

Our basket-mates often complain that we wake them up at night but, like all sloths, the only noises we make are little high pitched squeaks, so we tell them to stop being so sensitive.

Anyway, our peaceful, boring life came to a screeching halt when Slomo, another stuffed sloth, arrived. The Mom's big kids gave him to her for Christmas along with an Adoption Certificate that says she is the mom of a real live little sloth that fell out of a tree and now lives in a zoo. Mom put Slomo in our basket while she was cleaning up after Christmas and that's when things got a little bit crazy. I was just dozing off to sleep when she plopped him right on top of my head! That's when I heard him say, "Sorry, man!" as he climbed off me and snuggled between me and Slip. He was speaking English, not Slothish, which is the official Sloth language!

SLOMO™

Slip, Shee Shee and I climbed out of our basket and hung out with him on the sofa to listen to his story

Chapter II
SLOMO JOINS THE FAMILY

"Sorry to drop in on you like that!" he said.
"My name is Thlomo, it's actually spelled
S L O M O but because I haven't learned to
pronounce my "S's" yet I call myself 'Thlomo'.
I am a 3 toed thloth and come from a rainforest
in Costa Rica where I lived with my mom.
One day, while we were cuddling in our tree,
I lost my balance and fell way, way down to the
ground below.

I was rescued by a kind human who took me to an animal hospital and then to a zoo. I stayed there until the Mom's big kids came to get her adoption certificate. They took me, in my thtuffed form, to live here with you. The real Thlomo hugged me and said, "Before they put you in the gift bag, close your eyes and I will sprinkle some magic sloth spirit over you. That way you will always have a part of me deep down in your heart and soul."

"So here I am! Now tell me – what do you guys do for fun? There was a TV in the animal hospital and I learned a lot about little peoples' games. The next time thome kids come over here I'm going to play with them!"

"You can't do that!" I said. "No way Big People are going to let you play with their kids, especially since they don't even know you're alive!"
"Don't worry, I'll figure something out! But right now I'm thuper hungry! Where can a guy get thome flowers around here? Or at least a tasty piece of bark and a couple of wild berries?"

Chapter III
IT'S PARTY TIME!

Now it's Thlomo's turn to tell you the story:

Months passed and finally the Mom had a birthday party for one of the Little People. Everything was pretty much out of control which meant it was a perfect time for me to try to blend in: little kids were running in and out of sprinklers; bigger ones were shrieking and laughing as they threw water balloons at each other; and the smallest kids were bouncing on a trampoline. There was even a pony and a llama to ride. No one even noticed when I came lopping along!

HAPPY
BIRTHDAY

I showed one of the girls, Emmy, how to hang upside down in a tree.

She tried to drink her strawberry smoothie at the same time which didn't work out so well. It spilled all over her face and poured into her hair. "Look at what you made me do!" she yelled. "Look at my hair! It's all sticky!" "Your hair looks beautiful", I said. "Stop it, Slomo", she yelled.

Humans should try rubbing green moss on their hair like sloths do!

I played basketball with J.R. and Luke, two of the biggest boys. Kids named Ralphie, Endora and Vera were on the other team.

"Slomo - fast break!" my teammates shouted when I got the ball. I don't even know what that word "fast" means but I tried my best to get to the other side of the court and I think it's mean to call me a slow poke just because it took me fifteen minutes to get there! "Slomo's a slow poke, Slomo's a slow poke!", they teased me in a sing-song voice.

Humans should not make fun of others.

Next I played baseball with JJ, Jack and Brady.

When it was my turn at bat, boy did I ever smack that ball with my super strong arms! Running around the bases took a little while, though. By the time I got to home plate they had left the field and were eating birthday cake with everyone else.

Humans should be more patient with one another.

Then I went inside where some kids' moms
were drinking bubbly drinks and watching a
movie called   "Beaches".

They stared at me with angry faces because
while they were crying I was smiling. "I can't
help my face!" I thought to myself.

Humans shouldn't judge
others for how they look.

SLOMO

I knew the party was over when one of the neighbors who wasn't even invited started shouting, "What is that thing? I'm going to call the police!" "How rude!" I thought.

Humans should mind their own business!

The next day the Mom decided that it would be better for everyone if she brought me back to the zoo. I was excited to get back to my "alive" self but before I left I shared some of my favorite sloth wisdom with the Big and Little People:

EMBRACE YOUR INNER SLOTH:

Be authentic – no one does you better than you

Accept yourself – you are beautifully and perfectly made

Accept others – so are they!

Some things are better done slowly, like munching on a beautiful, pink, hibiscus flower

Slow down and look around even if it means you're the last one to reach the finish line

Always be smiling!

THE END

www.ingramcontent.com/pod-product-compliance
Lightning Source LLC
Chambersburg PA
CBHW041420300726

48981CB00007B/351